DEFINABLE AS SUNLIGHT
Issue n° 16 — Summer 2021

PART 1

Cover star MOSES SUMNEY is photographed by Kennedi Carter in Asheville, North Carolina.

PART 2

Sabahattin Ali's 1941 novel *Kürk Mantolu Madonna*, or *Madonna in a Fur Coat*, is processed in three completely different ways.

    Writers of various stripes elaborate on: the last sentence, Berlin Botanical Gardens, the knit vest, Lützowstraße, backgammon, soap manufacturing, a fur coat, cabbagey whiff, indescribable torrents of emotion in galleries, Ahmed Mithat Efendi, deliciously dry Rhein wine, the sitting room, body language, Bavarian outfits, an academy of fine arts, and beer halls.

Turkish artist Deniz Orkus kindly provides this issue's endpapers with her mixed-media work *Moments and Memories* (2019).

The technology of the book was invented to deal with otherwise loose and messy pages, as this picture by JASCHI KLEIN reminds.

PAGE NUMBERS

All books contain the same thing (besides whatever else they contain). All books tell a story that goes like this:

1

2

3

4

Eventually it stops. It contains no tension, and offers no surprises; the reader would prefer it if a '47' didn't spring in when they're expecting an '18'. There are certain conventions — odd on the right, even on the left — that are essentially unbearable if broken.

The first books didn't have page numbers. They were introduced by an innovative scribe or monk (no one knows who) to make it easier to find a passage in a text, and became widespread after around 1500. At some point they became so entrenched that for most readers, even if they rarely 'use' them, it's uncomfortable for them to be absent.

Page numbers are curious. They're the only thing on the page that the author didn't write. Like the clock on the wall or the lines on the road, they are meant to indicate rather than interfere. Which would be an achievable goal if their progression wasn't, like the ticking of said clock, so disquieting in its relentlessness.

Doesn't every reader feel a very basic glee, completely at odds with a supposedly intellectual activity, for the fact of the page number getting bigger and bigger? Don't they commit silent calculations as to their page-per-minute speed, and yearn to accelerate, like some motorhead from the '50s? Don't they, compulsively and often, turn to the very back of the book to check the final page number so as to longingly compare it with the one they're on? Strangest of all, don't they demonstrate this brute desire to 'win' — to just get to the end of a string of integers — even when they're actually enjoying the book?

As the figure below communicates, this is the fifth page of the issue. It contains sixty-eight pages in total, as they all have since issue ten, when we increased the total from sixty-six. Most are numbered. Please take a moment to appreciate those numbers' sturdy reliability. Please don't forget to look above them as well.

THE HAPPY READER
Bookish Magazine
Issue n° 16 — Summer 2021

The Happy Reader is
a collaboration between
Penguin Books and
Fantastic Man

EDITOR-IN-CHIEF
Seb Emina

ART DIRECTOR
Tom Etherington

MANAGING EDITOR
Maria Bedford

EDITORIAL DIRECTORS
Jop van Bennekom
Gert Jonkers

PICTURE RESEARCH
Frances Roper

PRODUCTION
Katy Banyard

DESIGN CONCEPT
Jop van Bennekom
Helios Capdevila

MARKETING
Liz Parsons

BRAND DIRECTOR
Sam Voulters

MARKETING DIRECTOR
Ingrid Matts

PUBLISHER
Stefan McGrath

CONTRIBUTORS
Liz Johnson Artur, Aaron
Ayscough, Tim Blanks, Kennedi
Carter, Banu Cennetoğlu,
Stephen Curtis, Sevil Delin,
Rob Doyle, Clym Evernden,
Kaya Genç, Richard Godwin,
Jan Kedves, Hilal Isler, Jordan
Kelly, Jamie MacRae, Rosa
Rankin-Gee, Viviane Sassen,
Ayşegül Sert, David Selim
Sayers, Elif Shafak, Jia
Tolentino, Julie Verhoeven

THANK YOU
Magnus Åkesson, Rebecca Lee,
Penny Martin, Caroline Pretty,
Anna Wilson

Penguin Books
20 Vauxhall Bridge Road
London SW1V 2SA

info@thehappyreader.com
www.thehappyreader.com

SNIPPETS

Diary column restocked with warm and sunny literary news

KIT — Tennis tournament? Business meeting? There are specialised items of clothing available. Reading a book? Not so much. However, the US-based on- and offline retailer Book/Shop proposes and indeed sells clothes designed especially for readers. These include the 'book jacket' (a sort of workers' jacket but with large rectangular pockets for you-know-what) and a refined category of pyjamas called a 'reading suit'.

PIONEERS — The National Cowboy Poetry Gathering, normally a late-winter occurrence in the city of Elko, Nevada, was forced to move proceedings online this year. Hardly the cowboy spirit, you might think. But actually, the whole programme went gallopingly well, from keynote speech 'Philosophers on Horseback' to live-streamed sets by poets and musicians, such as Navajo duo the Martin Sisters.

SUBLIME — A sculptural form called *Idiom*, which uses books and mirrors to create the illusion of an infinite to-be-read pile, can be viewed in the foyer of Prague Municipal Library. It was created by Matej Kren, an artist who loves erecting literary structures: other works by the 62-year-old include a highbrow cubicle called *Book Cell*.

WORMISH — To describe someone as a hardcore reader in English the term is bookworm, but what about in other languages? In Arabic we meet the book moth. In French and Spanish it's a library rat. Norwegians speak approvingly of the reading horse, the Finnish of the chapter maggot. Yet the bookworm is globally rampant, showing up in languages as mutually remote as Hindi, Russian, Farsi and Dutch.

HOOP — Basketball players with book clubs: it's a thing. Golden State Warriors' Stephen Curry has one focusing on books telling stories about people who transcend expectations; and the reading circle of Ekpe Udoh, alumnus of Utah Jazz and Beijing Ducks, embraces everything from the literary fiction of Colson Whitehead to the chronic page-turners of John Grisham.

HOT TAKE — Overheard in a bookshop in Paris: 'The most passive-aggressive word in the English language is "Congratulations".'

BIBLITECTURE — A new library in the Chinese province of Hainan is described by its architects MAD as a 'wormhole library' thanks to its futuristic appearance, resembling a curved spaceship of glass and white concrete with several ovoid holes right through the middle. Located in downtown Haikou on the island of Hainan, it will contain 10,000 books plus cosy seating with views of the Qiongzhou Strait.

BOOK FIRST — The phenomenon of the library-themed hotel, while in no way to be discouraged, has slowly but surely become a bit of a hospitality trope. But how about flipping the concept on its head? The recently-opened Book and Bed Tokyo is books first, rooms second; an 'accommodation bookstore' in which customers can browse titles in comfy nooks before falling asleep in the establishment if the mood takes them.

NEW U — Gruff singer Jimbo Mathus, of bands including Squirrel Nut Zippers, was in fact born with the surname 'Mathis'. He tweaked it in homage to William Faulkner, a favourite author from Mathus's hometown of Oxford, Mississippi. 'I changed the spelling many decades ago,' he tells The Happy Reader in a correspondence. 'Faulkner added the "u" to his name, which was originally "Falkner". He thought it looked more "British" and would add a sophisticated element to his name in print.'

SALACITY — Legendary fashion designer Rick Owens is gearing up to reread the complete plays of Tennessee Williams. 'I've read everything he ever did,' Owens tells The Happy Reader over a video call, 'and I think it's time to start reading him again. I remember how incredibly salacious he could be. There's cannibalism, there's ruptured colons... He's the most salacious of the salacious, but poetic and beautiful.'

WATCHING — The death mask of British Romantic poet John Keats, who died from tuberculosis in 1821, has sold at auction for £12,500. Keats was just 25 when he passed, his likeness at death preserved (as then the fashion) using a plaster cast. This latest sale, to Romantics professor Adeline Johns-Putra, was of a first-degree copy of one of two originals, both of which are now lost. Another Keats mask is held at Princeton University, whose death-mask collection also includes those of Leo Tolstoy, Walt Whitman, Dante Gabriel Rossetti and many more!

STOIC — Assuming normal life is indeed back by then, this year's 'Stoicon: The Modern Stoicism Conference' will take place in Toronto on 23 October. Events exploring the ancient philosophical discipline (encapsulated in the books of Seneca, Epictetus and Marcus Aurelius) will include a lecture on Stoic mindfulness, an appearance from a Stoic stand-up comedian, and a talk entitled 'Stoicism and Star Trek: Is Doctor Spock a Stoic?'

Much of the world agrees: MOSES SUMNEY's second album, *Græ*, was one of the standout records of 2020, its twenty tracks offering a poignant and enigmatic soundtrack to the strangest of times, the loneliest of years. Moses is as intense and chimerical as his singing voice. Of course, he's a big reader as well. His favourite books, as this interview-slash-pusuit-of-the-sublime reveals, are often about new ways to form an identity, to break out of tired old modes of living and become, once and for all, one's true unabridged self.

MOSES SUMNEY

In conversation with
JIA TOLENTINO

Portraits by
KENNEDI CARTER

MOSES SUMNEY
(19-05-90)

Born in: San Bernardino, California. Moved (aged 10) to: Accra, Ghana. Moved (aged 16) to: Riverside, California. Now lives in: Asheville, North Carolina. Studied: poetry, creative writing, theatre. Early jobs: wellness blogger, music writer, pizza marketer. Albums: *Aromanticism* (2017), *Græ* (2020). Collaborators include: Michael Chabon, Solange Knowles, Taiye Selasi, Sufjan Stevens. Height: 6' 4".

LOS ANGELES AND ASHEVILLE

I open a window on my computer and Moses Sumney appears — commandingly handsome, muscular in a black button-up shirt, shoulder-length locs tied up over a bleach-blond undershave, his demeanour as warm and expansive as the polluted, golden Los Angeles light that bursts through the greenery behind him.

I've felt all sorts of ways about Sumney's work ever since the summer night in 2017 that I was sitting in a dive bar, drinking piña coladas, and a friend of mine told me I had to — 'like tonight, I really mean it, you really have to' — listen to this artist Moses Sumney, this song of his called 'Doomed'. On the walk home I put the song through my headphones and felt overpowered by a sort of simultaneity that comes with genius in music, in writing, in any other art form: a pristine clarity, expressing oceanic weight. Since then, Sumney has been an artist whose body of work I've felt sure I'll be relying on for succour well into the future — like Social Security if such a thing could be trusted, like those shocking, bold, vulnerable all-night conversations you luck into every once in a while with friends who live far away. When Sumney sent over, in advance of our conversation, a list of books and essays that had been meaningful to him (see p. 27), I wasn't surprised to find several works I loved, a handful I was exhilarated to read for the first time, and a through line of uncompromising intellect and vision. In *Aromanticism*, his 2017 album, and then the double LP *Græ*, which came out in 2020, Sumney models complex original thinking, both sonically and lyrically — a refusal of given questions, an invention of deeper ones, a yearning for new tones, new forms of coexistence. And for all the ethereal beauty in Sumney's music, it's funny too. There's an irony and a wryness to his writing that emerges with special force in his live performances; it bursts forward as we talk over Zoom.

Sumney and I speak again, a week later, and this time he's returned to his home in Asheville, North Carolina. Sumney has stacked some of his favourite books next to the computer — we spend a lot of time reading passages to each other — and he shows me the woods just outside his back door. The two conversations are combined here, but the first one begins when he tells me:

MOSES: It's a bit weird to talk to you, because I feel like I know you, which is such an internet-age thing.

JIA: I'm having a similar feeling. I've listened to your voice so much, so closely, for so long. I feel like I've spent time in your mind. And now we're here, talking.

M: Yes, and because I've read so much of your writing and watched a few of your interviews — it's so interesting to have the experience of interfacing with someone through a screen but not actually speaking to them, but then, now, interfacing with them through a screen *while speaking to them.* So that's kind of an interesting moment I'm having. I will have you know I am feeling very, very much like an imposter. I'm feeling like, 'Whoa, okay, we're gonna talk about books. I'm doing this with an *author.*' It's actually quite an intense feeling.

J: I'm absolutely thrilled to get to talk to you about books. It's rare to be able to speak to someone you admire, whose work you admire, about something meaningful that is not specifically their work or their self, but that sits between those two things. But before we start talking about books, there are two things I have to tell you. First, you played that show in Brooklyn at Public Records on March 9, 2020 — a date I remember because it was the last show that I went to before... you know. Right now it feels like the last show I'll ever go to in my life.

M: [laughs] As much as it sucks that everything's shut down, I'm kind of happy to hear that. I'm like, 'That's sick.' Not literally.

J: And second, in August, I was literally listening to your album when I birthed my baby. It was hour twenty-four of the process and I needed to relax into the situation, to reinhabit my body in a different way. So I put on your album, and I did relax: I ended up falling asleep. And then I woke up and my doctor was hovering over me in her surgical hairnet, the operating theatre lights were up, her hand was all the way in me, and she was like, 'Okay girl, let's go.' And that final push happened in about ten minutes and suddenly the baby was on my chest

In the beginning, composition
is a private matter.

and 'Me in 20 Years' was playing and my boyfriend was just sobbing. It was one of the wildest experiences I think I'll ever have in my life.

M: Oh my God. I mean, I'm honoured. What intense music to bring a child into the world to. There is so much poetry in that. It's really blowing me away. Also, you picked a perfect time to have a child, didn't you?

J: Yeah. No FOMO. Everyone else is stuck in the house just like me.

M: I feel that way a lot about not living in LA or New York, because I have a lot of FOMO about LA. But now, no one's doing anything. So I'm good.

J: At the same time, reading other interviews with you, it sounds like it's always been self-evidently worthwhile to you to be in Asheville and have that space.

M: I have always known really acutely what is not serving me. So as much as I enjoy going out, I never look back at a night out and think, 'Wow, that really impacted my life in a positive way.' I'm always like, 'Why the fuck was I hanging out with these people?' I know being at home and thinking will benefit me and my artistry much more.

J: I feel similarly, in that I can't really think unless I'm alone — but I'm also realising, this past year, how almost every interesting connection I've ever made around an idea has stemmed from some in-person experience. I've felt static as a result, kind of foggy. Or maybe it's just the baby. We're now in month eleven of quarantine. How is it treating you?

M: I know I'm not the first to say this, but as an introvert, I've really had a transcendent quarantine. I had been living in Asheville for two years when lockdown happened and I had never been there for longer than three weeks. So it was like, 'Oh cool, I have to be at home and clean every day and learn how to cook.' That was all really fun. I got to read.

J: So you haven't gotten sick of being alone.

M: No. I want more of it. I am not sick of it. I feel stimulated when I have conversations with people I care about, and it's enough. It's enough for me. I don't get sick of being alone. I do get lonely, but I don't get sick of being alone.

J: What was the most transcendent reading experience you had in quarantine?

M: It was probably reading *Giovanni's Room*.

1.

J: First time?

M: Yes. I don't think I would have properly got it if I read it when I was younger. I would have missed some things. You've got to live a little.

J: What feeling did it leave you with?

M: Devastation, maybe. Devastation but also seen. I feel that as I navigate the world I'm seeing all the in-betweens, constantly weaving between the geometric lines, and I felt like Baldwin was seeing his characters and seeing the world in a similar way.

J: In rereading that book for our conversation, I was struck in a new way by the end, when David is looking in the mirror and he's taking off his clothes and imagining Giovanni awaiting execution. There's this line: Baldwin writes, *But the key to my salvation which cannot save my body is hidden in my flesh.' And the paragraph right afterwards — it reaches this unbelievable register. 'I move at last from the mirror and begin to cover that nakedness which I must hold sacred, though it be never so vile, which must be scoured perpetually with the salt of my life. I must believe, I must believe, that the heavy grace of God, which has brought me to this place, is all that can carry me out of it.*

M: Wow. Wow.

J: Yeah. I guess there's nothing we can say after that.

M: I'm just like, well!

J: Anyway!

M: No, but it's so good to meditate on this. It's not an image we see in literature, or in media at all — a man standing in front of a mirror and wondering what this all means. I was blown away by it. That line — 'I move... and begin to cover that nakedness which I must hold sacred' — I think of it in two ways. That the body or the nakedness or the truth is something to be preserved and guarded, protected. But the double-edged sword of that fact is that his nakedness is covered with impurity — with the impurity of the social expectation to cover up that nakedness. Does that make sense?

J: Yes, completely. It's there again in the line 'scoured perpetually with the salt of my life'. There's this possibility raised — that maybe the thing that's corrosive is also purifying. Anyway. Let's back away from the extremity of human existence for a minute. Can you tell me an early sensory memory you have of reading?

M: Two things. My love for reading was sparked when I was around eight or nine. I'd go to the library with my parents, who lived

in San Bernardino, California. Every Saturday I'd get a bunch of books. I'd read twenty books a week. My parents were like, 'You need a life.' The other thing I think of — I was around eleven or twelve. We moved to Ghana when I was ten, and one of the things my parents did was collect things from their church circles in America to distribute in the village. We had boxes of books in this really dusty room at the bottom level of the house. So I would go into that room because there wasn't a library anywhere near where we lived, and I would just go through the books. There was this strong smell of this kind of Ghanaian dust. The book I really loved around that age was *Where the Red Fern Grows*. It was the first book that I wanted to hold and clutch in that way.

2.

J: Ugh, that book. Two of the best all-time literary dogs. And it's devastating! It's funny how all kids' stories are endlessly rehearsing abandonment and death. It's interesting how we crave that when we're little; we need some way to understand it. I think about how *The Boxcar Children* was literally four orphans living in the woods, making a home out of garbage. And here's me like, 'Yes!! Amazing!!'

M: Suffer, suffer, suffer!

3.

J: Another question about childhood: we both grew up in very religious environments. Did you grow up reading a lot of the Bible?

M: Oh yes.

J: What were you attracted to in the Bible, thinking about it as literature? I used to get bored in church and read Revelations and trip out. Or sometimes I'd sneak looks at the sexy stuff in Song of Solomon.

M: Well, we were not *allowed* to read Revelations, because it was like, 'Not yet! You're not ready for this yet!' But I sometimes flipped through it, like, 'Wait, *what's* gonna happen to me?' The parts that I loved reading — I think I secretly loved reading Proverbs. I would protest all day long, don't get me wrong, from having to read the Bible. But the wisdom in Proverbs I really loved. And when I wanted to be rebellious, I loved reading Song of Solomon too. It felt so taboo. It felt like it was adding a complexity to my Christianity that wasn't actually being addressed in real life. We were never addressing sensuality, and childhood is so inherently sensual. Also, the first five books of the Bible were written by Moses. So my own childhood narcissism made it so I was super into those books. Like, 'Yeah I wrote that!'

J: What's the earliest literary representation of sex that really took hold for you?

M: I think it's *The Thorn Birds*. Whoa. I haven't thought about this in a long time. It's a book about a priest who — I think — has to choose between love and priesthood. But he meets this young girl, actually a probably inappropriately young girl, and falls in love with her. And there's a crazy sex scene in it. It's actually pornographic. I just read it over and over and over as a child. I remember kind of hiding in my room and just reading it again and reading it again. I think I returned the book, and I ripped the pages out that had all the graphic stuff in it. Did your parents address sex or sexuality with you or was it the kind of thing you never talked about it?

4.

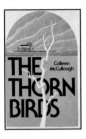

J: My mom sat me down when I was four or five, and she drew me a diagram and was like, 'This is what sex is.' And I was like, 'That sounds like it hurts.' And she was like, 'Yeah Jia, totally, we hate to do it.' And then we never discussed it again and of course I ended up living with my college boyfriend when I was seventeen. What about your parents?

M: We literally never talked about it. It wasn't even like, 'Kids, don't have sex.' It was just like... I think they just kind of hoped we wouldn't find out about it.

J: Did you write stories as a kid? And if you did, were there any particular things you tended to write about again and again? I would write about girls who opened a door in their closet and found themselves in a new world.

M: I always wrote about people with powers. I would always write about a kid who would discover a gemstone and it would change his DNA, or I would write this story about a guy whose power was that he could dissolve at any given moment. I wrote about powers and escape.

J: I'm curious about how you related to romantic narratives in books, in movies, growing up. *Aromanticism* raises questions around absence, around the primacy of romance in culture, in this phenomenally multivalent way — in a romantic way, even.

5.

M: I think when you're being young, and you're being presented with narratives about how life is supposed to be — I didn't necessarily explicitly say, 'Oh but not me, not for me.' I think you try to figure out how you're going to sit into that box. So for me, as a child who was very introverted — I did not have many friends, I spent most of my time alone, reading and writing and listening to music — I did have romantic inclinations and romantic desires. I had a really creative imagination, so fantasy was such a huge part of my childhood, and romantic fantasy was a *huge* part of my adolescence. What I was not able to do was parse out which of those were solely my own, versus what was being laid out as the path of normalcy. Am I having

romantic feelings because I've been told I'm supposed to, or are they innate? And I think it was both. But I always had this kind of sense of otherness. Alienation was a part of my childhood anyway, as a first-generation American, as a child who moved to Ghana. It was baked into every aspect of my life. I think it just happened that somewhere along the line I realised that my own romantic orientation was much more complex than what I was finding in any kind of narrative in the media, film or books.

J: Are there any books that have articulated what you were getting at with *Aromanticism* in regards to absence and searching and playing with the idea of romantic love? Have you since read anything that's captured the complexity of how you felt about romantic love?

6.

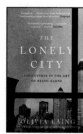

M: *Giovanni's Room*, honestly. Or *The Lonely City* by Olivia Laing: even though much of it is not about romance, it came close to addressing or touching on how I felt about the complexity of loneliness, which is kind of intrinsic to *Aromanticism*. I think what I *was* looking for while writing *Aromanticism* were narratives that address the possibility that love is just not in the cards for some people. It seems like the possibility of that truth was perhaps too dark, too stark, for some people to contend with. Even in my own reality, and in that album, I was not so much trying to present this idea of 'This is the way it is — this is the way I am.' But I wanted to propose questions around absence, around longing. I thought that there was a real gap in that conversation.

J: We could talk forever, I think, about how frustrating it is to encounter the kind of critical reading whose primary lens is 'Let's use this as a decoder ring on this person.'

M: I hate it, I hate it, I hate it. And just as someone who's not necessarily writing autobiography, I think that there is a piece of you in everything you write, even if you're writing about other people's perspectives. Of course. But I think it is a shame when people look at your work and then have an idea or insist that they have an idea of who you are as a person. I think that in itself is very alienating. A piece of work is a snapshot of a moment in time. It's the collection of thoughts and ideas and you might hit send and the next day you have a new thought or idea.

J: Right. You use yourself and your instincts as a way to get into the things you're trying to think about. And then it's read as 'Oh, this person is using these ideas to express something about *themselves*', when actually it's very much the opposite. So, you went to UCLA, and you were a creative writing major.

M: Yes — my emphasis was in poetry.

J: How did you find the institutional creative writing experience?

M: I did actually love the peer critique of workshop. It was soul-crushing and terrifying. I'd hidden my writing my whole life because I was kind of shy, and I didn't come from a very encouraging family — to do anything creative was like 'no way'. But you know, the experience was also alienating, because I realised my kind of perspective on literature was deeply not canonised. I was reading Faulkner for the first time and reading the Beat poets for the first time, basically everything that white guys thought were great, being like, 'What the fuck is this?'

J: Every year in high school — white man after white man. I was radicalised by the boredom of having to read *All Quiet on the Western Front* and *A Separate Peace* back-to-back.

7.

M: I hated *The Catcher in the Rye*.

J: Oh, yeah, I hate that book so much.

M: I was like, 'What is everyone talking about?' Like, who cares? I just don't care.

J: It's an iconic fake-deep artefact.

8.

M: It's so fake-deep. Where's the revelation here? I don't see it. Like I said, Faulkner, I was annoyed. I was impressed by Faulkner, but I was annoyed. But what I loved was the Romantic poets. I found that really gorgeous. I really loved William Blake.

J: Yeah. Blake is really trippy. Those poets — there's so much of the sublime.

M: Sublime is the right word. And anything that romanticised nature, anything that was transcendental, I really appreciated it. I absolutely loved Thoreau. I felt like it kind of spoke to my spirituality, or whatever spirituality survived after I ran away from Christianity. I loved anything that allowed me to regard nature as larger than us, to connect our own feelings to it.

9.

J: That's exactly what happened to me. I ran away from the conservative church, but there are remnants. Any time I do a hallucinogen around a tree, I'm like, 'It's God!'

M: The tree is God!

J: Any time I start thinking about how many things are growing simultaneously on the planet while I'm high I feel the same feeling

I felt when I was little and believed in God. Nature has become the receptacle for any sense of the divine for me.

M: I really believe that and I really believe in that. I moved to the mountains because I wanted to have that feeling, I wanted to have that feeling that Henry David Thoreau felt. And I think that it is God. I think she is God.

J: Whatever makes the tree grow is functionally as close to God as I am interested in getting, kind of.

M: Absolutely.

J: So, you deleted your Twitter recently. Has your brain felt better since doing it?

M: Yes. Oh God, yes. Where do I even start? I know for a fact the internet has made me dumber. I know that for a fact. I remember reading that book *The Shallows* about eight years ago, even before I got on Twitter. And the pathways of my brain are just fucking dirt roads now.

10.

J: Have you read *How to Do Nothing?*

M: No, but I bought it. It's on my bookshelf.

J: It's a good one. It gave me an existential crisis. It's one of the few books I read where I was instantly changed.

M: Really?

11.

J: Yeah. But my brain is still fucked because of the internet.

M: It's really bad and it's really sad. The thing I most wanted to curb was the involuntary unconscious habit of opening Twitter. I'll be in the middle of typing an email and then I'm reading a tweet, and I don't even remember typing in the website, you know?

J: You recently posted an Instagram of yourself naked in front of a waterfall. In the caption you wrote that you were thinking about pleasure and joy and nature, and where they intersect with decolonisation. What prompted these thoughts, at that moment?

M: Oh, I'll tell you exactly. I just spent a month in Ghana, and the fact is, there is nowhere in the world I can go and just *be* and not be made to think of my difference. I had just gotten my dual citizenship — I've always only been an American citizen. And I went to the passport office, went to take the photo, and they're like, 'You have to take out your piercings.' Their whole thinking was, you cannot have a Ghanaian passport and show up in the world with all this shit on your face, because what is the Western world going to think about

Located 650 metres above sea level, the climate in Asheville is pretty damn cool.

us? There was this post-colonial respectability that had to be upheld. I ended up being in this thirty-minute argument, like, 'Do you even know the history of body modifications? Do you know the history of piercings?' There is this staunch idea of traditionalism but it doesn't extend to the pre-colonial. And then I was at this waterfall. I had spent three hours hiking, and there was no one there except white tourists. Ghana is a coastal country, but people really don't know how to swim, people don't go to the beach to swim. People are afraid to get in the water. What does that mean? Ghana, as you read in *Homegoing*, is where a lot of slaves were brought through, and that's part of the reason people are still afraid to get in the water. But there is this idea of respectability and what it means to be civilised. People don't want to be caught in waterfalls getting all dirty and stuff. There's this concept of: *we are beyond that*. So I was thinking about decolonisation, and about self-policing. Black people can be the guardians of colonialism; we're the guardians of patriarchy in a lot of ways. There doesn't have to be an actual oppressor present in the room for the rules to still be disseminated and protected.

12.

J: How long have you been engaged in the project of decolonisation, in your own life, and what are the books that have guided you in this?

M: I feel like I started quite late, like in my late teens and then my early twenties. I always understood about myself that I could see the truth but I also feel like I was seeing the wrong truths for most of my life. To be more specific, I think I had a lot of criticism for Black people all of my life. My life was made very difficult by Black people, and so I was able to be like, 'No! We need to welcome people who are different.' But in my late teens and early twenties, I was able to zoom out and recognise that colonisation and post-imperialism and patriarchy and the patriarchy of whiteness specifically were the reason there were intra-community problems. In terms of books, I think *The Autobiography of Malcolm X* was a huge one for me in my early twenties. One of my favourite books. Also we have the same birthday, by the way.

13.

J: What's your birthday?

M: May 19th. Me, Malcolm X and Grace Jones.

J: Wow. If I can go back to *Homegoing*, which I hadn't read until early in quarantine, actually: tell me more about how that book was meaningful to you?

M: It was the fact that it begins with a pre-colonial narrative. It was like a lightbulb came on for me. So much of African history is passed on orally, so we have so few texts from that time. And obviously, as a Ghanaian, I'm thinking about the diasporic movement, having to make the connection of Black people in America to Black people in Africa.

J: I was just reading Silvia Federici's *Caliban and the Witch* and thinking about how often I fall into the trap of thinking that capitalism and patriarchy have existed forever and that we've just recently gained the language to repudiate them — forgetting the extent to which these modes of living were formed in a specific material context and then maintained through violence. In *Homegoing*, you get to see how violent that transition and maintenance was. And then in something like Marlon James's *Black Leopard, Red Wolf*, you get a pre-colonial world reimagined altogether. I know you're a fan of Marlon's work, as am I. Don't you think — it's so musical?

14.

M: Yeah. Rhythmic. But when I read his work, sometimes I feel like I'm looking at a painting. I'm looking at a Rothko painting really up close. I don't always understand every word of his vernacular or the grammatical structure of it but he understands how to communicate feeling, and how to communicate an image so strongly. Or sound, even. And it does feel that he's looking for ways to dismantle canonical language — this really kind of colonial standard where everything has to be proper. It's so powerful to see how something that is so cerebral can create so much motion, so much feeling.

15.

J: How do you choose what you want to read? How do you go about buying books?

M: I have a lot of books. I'm kind of a compulsive book buyer. I don't know if you do this — I buy books that I might not read for a couple years.

J: I think that's the best way to be. You have to read books at the right moment. I feel like it does the book a disservice otherwise — to not meet it in the right place.

M: Totally. I also have a bunch of books that I've started and I'm like, 'This doesn't feel like the right time for this book.'

J: I think reading something at the wrong time is like being hungry but not eating what you want to eat. It's a waste of appetite.

M: I think, also, for the types of stuff I read, there is a real synthesis between the soul and the mind. I think that at different points in our lives our souls have different appetites — and these appetites are influenced by what's going on in our lives. So it actually is quite metaphysical, how I'm going to connect with any book at any given moment.

16.

J: You read *Close to the Knives* recently, by David Wojnarowicz. I don't know how to pronounce it. I'm looking it up. Voy-na-ro-vich.

M: I've been told this like four times but I also can't pronounce it. Homeboy's book, yes.

J: What was the appetite that was being fulfilled when you read it?

M: I was surprised to find a little bit of an academic bent to it, because I always like that — and also such soulfulness. I think I'm always looking for someone who is able to look at the world and see through all of the bullshit, to see the inherent beauty of it and the brutality of it, and to recognise the ways in which those two things are connected. The way David is able to tease the beauty out of what would be considered very abject — he has such a longing that he carries in the world as someone who's an outcast. He's trying to fill the void of that longing with an abject physicality that's probably hurting him, but he sees it as beautiful, and it's crushing.

J: I read the entire book last night, wanting to talk to you about it — I need to read it again later, slower. But the scene with him and the guy outside the truck stop, and the sweat on their bodies, and they pause as the cars go by. The delicacy of that was devastating — the tenderness of having to stop. I flagged one line, where he writes *I want to throw up because we're supposed to quietly and politely make house in this killing machine called Ametrica and pay taxes to support our own slow murder and I'm amazed that we're not running amok in the streets. That we can still be capable of gestures of loving after lifetimes of all of this.*

M: *That we can still be capable of gestures of loving after lifetimes of all of this.* Ugh.

J: This question, of what it means to be able to make space for tenderness along compromised lines... it's sort of like, why else are we alive?

M: It's interesting to think about David W— homeboy's experience with his family, his father. The terrible physical abuse. Like, that is our blueprint. The family is our foundation of where we learn about love. So I think he actually doesn't know how to divorce brutality and intimacy. That is the genesis of what it means to be cared for, for him. I found a passage I like — it's kind of long. He's talking about having sex with someone. *In loving him, I saw men encouraging each other to lay down their arms. In loving him, I saw small-town laborers creating excavations that other men spend their lives trying to fill. In loving him, I saw moving films of stone buildings; I saw a hand in prison dragging snow in from the sill. In loving him, I saw great houses being erected that would soon slide into the waiting and stirring seas. I saw him freeing me from the silences of the interior life.* What can you even say?

RECENT READS

A reading list of Moses's latest favourites spans an impressive range of subject matters, but with several strong motifs in view.

IDEA → SUBJECT

← SCREENPLAY (1979) by Syd Field — The three-act screenplay model was first identified in this filmmaking guide, which remains a perennial best-seller. To summarise: act one is 'the setup', act two is 'the confrontation', and act three is 'the resolution'. Just fill in the specifics, and off you go.

↓ HOMEGOING (2016) by Yaa Gyasi — The title of the debut novel by Ghanaian-American author Yaa Gyasi is in reference to an old African-American belief that on death one's soul might return to Africa. The book follows two families from the eighteenth century to the twenty-first, along the way taking a clear-eyed look at West Africa's role in the slave trade.

'Flower Child' Surrenders. Detective and policewoman (r.) escort actress Valerie Solanas, 28, into E. 21st St. station to be booked in shooting of pop art movie man Andy Warhol at his 33 Union Square West office yesterday. Last night, Valerie surrendered to a cop in Times Square, allegedly admitting shooting, and saying: "I am a flower child." Warhol is in critical condition. His associate, Mario Amaya of London, also was shot. —Stories p. 3; other pics. centerfold

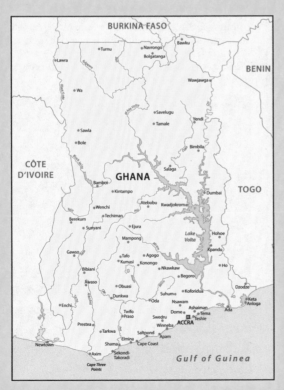

↑ SCUM MANIFESTO (1967) by Valerie Solanas — 'To be male is to be deficient, emotionally limited,' writes Valerie Solanas in *Scum Manifesto*. It argues for the overthrow of the money system, the institution of automation, and the destruction of the male sex. Mostly it argues for the destruction of the male sex, a male being essentially, writes Solanas, an incomplete female. It has remained influential. Any mention of *Scum Manifesto* is duty bound to acknowledge it'd never have gained such notoriety had she not shot the world's most famous artist. She confessed and went to prison; Andy Warhol survived but was never the same though he did later satirise Solanas in his film *Women in Revolt*.

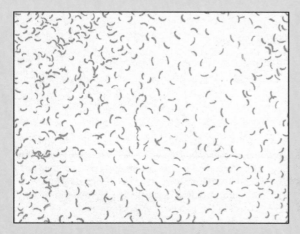

↑ THE PLAGUE (1947) by Albert Camus — If any book was trending in the early months of the pandemic, it was *The Plague*, Albert Camus' story of a contagion setting in, of its becoming entrenched in a community. The book has an allegorical level as well. See the publication date: the plague can be taken as straightforward illness but it can also be taken as fascist ideology. As time has passed, so have the meanings accumulated.

↑ CHELSEA GIRLS (1994) by Eileen Myles — What kind of book is *Chelsea Girls*? Structured as a series of essays, it's described in *The Paris Review* as a *Künstlerroman* or 'artists' novel'. The artist is Eileen Myles, a lesbian poet from Arlington, Massachusetts and the cumulative effect is a memoiristic tale of coming to terms with, and then embracing, all of the above. 'I mainly needed to say what I thought was real,' Myles commented recently.

↓ CLOSE TO THE KNIVES (1991) by David Wojnarowicz — The artist David Wojnarowicz was only 37 when he died from AIDS-related illnesses. He left behind an astonishing body of work. Known for his painting but working in other media as well, he moved in a New York-based circle of artists including Jean-Michel Basquiat, Nan Goldin and Keith Haring. This collection of autobiographical essays ensure his voice is still being heard thirty years after his death.

↓ TRICK MIRROR (2019) by Jia Tolentino — 'These essays are about the spheres of public imagination that have shaped my understanding of myself, of this country, of this era,' writes Tolentino introducing her acclaimed first collection. Subjects tackled include early and late internet culture, athleisure as a fetish, the mixtapes of DJ Screw, and, as per p. 21 of this interview, organised religion and its discontents.

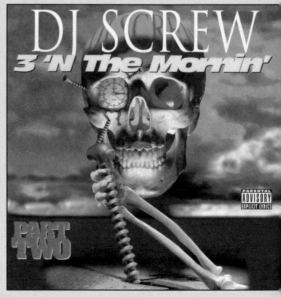

↓ IT'S HARD TO FIND A GOOD LAMP (1993 essay) by Donald Judd — An essay on the difference between art and design. 'The art of a chair is not its resemblance to art, but is partly its reasonableness, usefulness and scale as a chair,' writes the influential American artist.

↓ GIOVANNI'S ROOM (1956) by James Baldwin — Baldwin's stunning novel is centred around an affair between an American narrator, David, and an Italian barman, Giovanni. The book is, 'not so much about homosexual love,' said Baldwin in an interview in 1980, 'it is what happens if you are so afraid that you find you cannot love anybody.'

↑ THE COMMUNIST MANIFESTO (1848) by Karl Marx and Friedrich Engels — 'A spectre is haunting Europe,' begins *The Communist Manifesto* (isn't one always?). Few books are more famous, few books are more influential, yet the fame — or notoriety — doesn't often lead to the actual reading of it. Many feel they already know what they'll find here; they may be surprised.

↑ BLACK LEOPARD, RED WOLF (2019) by Marlon James — Having won the Booker prize for his sprawling modernist novel *A Brief History of Seven Killings*, Marlon James turned his talent in a different direction. This is a fantasy novel — first in a trilogy — that draws on African mythology, and for which film rights have been acquired by Michael B. Jordan aka *The Black Panther*'s supervillain, Erik Killmonger.

LESS RECENT READS

It's only with the benefit of time passing that we understand which books have had a real impact on us, like the titles on Moses's second reading list.

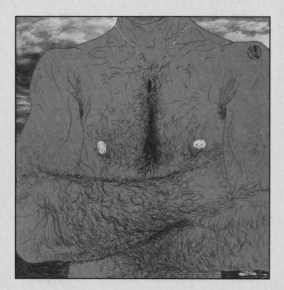

↑ CONFESSIONS OF A MASK (1949) by Yukio Mishima — 'For many years I claimed I could remember things seen at the time of my own birth.' Yukio Mishima, represented here in a classic portrait by designer Tadanori Yokoo, was one of the most important Japanese novelists of the twentieth century. This is the novel that made him famous: the story of a gay narrator trying to make his way, and conceal his identity, in imperial Japan.

↑ THE ARGONAUTS (2015) by Maggie Nelson — Jason's mythical ship the Argo serves as a totemic metaphor in Nelson's near-undefinable book (experi-mental essay? Fragmentary memoir? But often funnier than either of those sound) challenging old ideas of sex, motherhood, and what it means to be free.

↓ SISTER OUTSIDER (1984) by Audre Lorde — Fifteen essays and speeches on subjects including sexuality, feminism, motherhood, and the erotic versus the pornographic, which more than live up to the description Audre Lorde once gave for herself as a 'black lesbian feminist warrior poet'.

↓ ORLANDO (1928) by Virginia Woolf — 'I'm sick to death of this particular self. I want another.' Woolf's famous fictional biography is of a poet who lives for centuries, along the way turning from man to a woman. Orlando serves as an ambassador to Constantinople before marrying a gender non-conforming sea captain.

P. 29: Bridgeman Images. *Untitled*, 1980 © Judd Foundation ARS, NY and DACS, London 2021. Gift of Dr. Steven Conant in Memory of Mrs. H.L. Conant/Bridgeman Images; Photo Anthony Barboza/Getty Images; Photo Allstar Picture Library Ltd./Alamy. P. 30: *Illustration for 'Killed By Roses'. A Book Of Portraits Of Yukio Mishima*, 1969 by Tadanori Yokoo.

J: Yes. This passage. When I read the line about the hand dragging snow in from the sill —

M: In a prison.

J: I was like, 'I'm going to remember this image until the day I die.'

M: The other thing I really love about this book and his writing is: it made me think about the utility of anger. What it means to channel anger, but also what it means to not hide that anger. That was also quite radical for me. Because I often think, for minoritised people, we have to show up in the world not angry. We've come to know that if you show up in the world in certain spaces carrying your anger on your shoulders, all of your beauty and your humanity or even just the message that you are walking into the room can and will be discarded. If you're emotional, how can you be rational? But oftentimes anger is the most rational response to the world. So I just loved and appreciated not only his ability to harness his own anger but his commitment to sharing it. To being like, 'No, I am angry. That's the whole fucking point.'

J: I was struck by his anger too. Specifically, the way it was rooted in this ultimate fury that the structures of the world are making it so that we are here, alive, living in ways that hardly acknowledge the possibilities that are inherent to being human, the freedom and love we have a right to. He says something about not wanting to make it to your last day and realise that you just went along with the preconceived world.

M: I think this is what you're referencing. *There is something I want to see clearly, something I want to witness in its raw state. And this need comes from my sense of mortality. There is a relief in having this sense of mortality. At least I won't arrive one day at my eightieth birthday and at the eve of my possible death and only then realize my whole life was supposed to be somewhat a preparation for the event of death and suddenly fill up with rage because instead of preparation all I had was a lifetime of adaptation to the pre-invented world.*

J: The pre-invented world...

M: The pre-invented world!

J: There are so many connections underneath all of the books you've brought up: they are so much about the alienation produced by artificial ideas of power and normativity, and they all have this tremendous force of humanity trying to...

M: Push through.

Moses is open about his
innate shyness and wrote
a song called 'Lonely World'.
Photographic assistance:
Peyton Sickles. Grooming:
Kahlani Jackson.

J: Push through! You've also mentioned Audre Lorde's *Uses of the Erotic* before — another work that is all about unused and unacknowledged potential and power. Being able to touch electricity without fearing it. There's a line in that essay where she says, *... for the erotic is not a question only of what we do; it is a question of how acutely and fully we can feel in the doing. Once we know the extent we are capable of feeling that sense of satisfaction and completion, we can then observe which of our various life endeavors brings us closely to that fullness.*

17.

Audre Lorde

Uses of the Erotic:
The Erotic as Power

M: You know, I was actually also looking at my notes from when I read your book, and your essay on ecstasy I feel relates to what we're talking about right now. I'm going to pull up the quote, if you don't mind being put on the spot here. [laughs] When Jia Tolentino says, *I have been overpowered with ecstasy in religious settings, during bouts of hedonistic excess, on Friday afternoons walking sober in the park as the sun turns everything translucent gold... The fact that everything feels like God to me ensured that I would not remain a Christian. Church never felt much more like virtue than drugs did, and drugs never felt much more sinful than church.*

J: There's this question here — and it's there in Wojnarowicz's truck-stop sex — of pursuing something unmitigated, unmediated. The feeling of accessing that, however it manifests, is unmistakable, and it's nothing like the pre-invented world. It's rarely within the accepted structures of the world. Maybe it's *only* outside of these structures. I've understood this for some time but I'm trying to figure out more how to really run my life by these principles. Do you think you'll ever write a book?

M: I would definitely never write a novel. I don't really engage with the world in that way. But I miss writing essays, and if I had not become a musician I would probably be trying to write essays right now. Cultural criticism that weaves together gender and race studies and pop culture. Sometimes I'm like, it would be so fucking cool to write a book of essays.

J: You should!

M: I think if I was writing essays or I was writing some kind of cultural criticism, I would, in my opinion, be more bearable as a musician. There's so much cultural or social critique in my actual work, and I somehow turned my work into an outlet for all of these opinions... and then the interesting experiment has been how to synthesise my own sociocultural criticism with the interiority of my life. I enjoy my work, but sometimes it feels like too intellectual of an exercise. It would be nice to just write a song.

J: Are you moving more in that direction?

M: I am. Definitely. I've realised in the past few days — all of this thinking about eroticism and sensuality and the natural state of being I think is helping me actually weirdly get to this place of: sometimes a song can just be a song.

J: Can you describe your perfect reading experience?

M: I'm definitely in the mountains, in a cabin, there's a big window. I'm warm, and outside the window everything is lush and green and there's an expansive view I can see from just above the page. I like it being kind of like 5pm, depending on the season. The sun is probably setting. Everything is warm, inside and outside. There are reddish tones and hues bouncing off of things, shadows. Shadows are falling and moving. I love that as a setting. As for what I'm reading, I don't know — any of the books we've just talked about.

(END)

THE HAPPY
READER

When your colleague writes a book about the meaning of love... Here the spotlight shifts to MADONNA IN A FUR COAT, a classic novel from Turkey that's in perfect tune with the mood of the '20s.

This image: *Eifersucht* (1927) by László Moholy-Nagy

2.1
STORY OF A BOOK

One of the biggest literary blockbusters in Turkey in recent years is a curious romance from decades ago. It was published in the early '40s, only to be greeted with indifference, shunned by its author and more or less forgotten save for a network of word-of-mouth enthusiasm. Of late, however, *Madonna in a Fur Coat* is an explosive bestseller, an omnipresent artefact in readers' hands, one that has sold more than 2.5 million copies since being republished in 1998 and embraced by yet more fans after being translated into English in 2016. Sabahattin Ali's final novel is a paradox — a classic that's also contemporary, an old book that's mostly popular with the young — and the  question of how and why it went from underground legend to mass-market hit is tantalising, just like the layered narratives stashed within its pages.

The lightning-strike of meeting 'the one' is a crowd-pleasing theme, and Ali knows the melodramatic tricks — secret notebooks, missed encounters — that produce a proper page-turner. But the real magic, writes ELIF SHAFAK, is the way he uses all this to smuggle in an excitingly subversive worldview.

OF FINDING A LOVE STORY THAT I ACTUALLY LOVED

The first time I read *Madonna in a Fur Coat* I was a student in Ankara. The city was covered with a blanket of smog that winter, the air smelled of coal dust and roasted chestnuts, power cuts were common, and at night, sitting by candlelight, I secretly dreamed of becoming a writer. Back then, I kept a notebook where I wrote down my views on the female characters that I came across in Turkish novels and short stories. In so many of them women were either devoted mothers and exemplary wives, or dangerous seductresses and destroyers of family values, or elusive, dream-like figures, intended to serve as muses to male authors. I was beginning to suspect there was barely any other representation possible for women in early modern Turkish literature — that is, until I started reading Sabahattin Ali's deeply moving, quietly transformative novel.

Structured as a story within a story, *Madonna in a Fur Coat* centres upon an unusual love affair between Raif, a young Turkish Muslim man visiting Berlin for the first time, and a German Jewish artist, Maria. Raif has been sent to Germany by his father in the hope that he would learn soap manufacturing and help the family business to thrive. But it is art, literature and culture that the young man is really passionate about. As he walks the streets of Weimar Berlin, a shy and introverted *flâneur*, so we, the readers, traverse the same streets with him. Everything changes when Raif chances upon a painting, a self-portrait, by a mysterious artist: Maria Puder. He is profoundly moved not only by the beauty and unreachability of the woman in the painting but also by her aura of melancholy.

It will soon become evident that Maria is a strong character. Opinionated and independent, she exudes a self-confidence that Raif visibly lacks. While she is rational, wilful, unsentimental and pragmatic, he is almost the opposite in every sense: emotional, unassertive and tender-hearted, qualities that will only cause him problems when he returns to his motherland, Turkey, where men are expected to conform to a certain form of masculinity. A man regarded as 'effeminate' in a patriarchal land is bound to be misunderstood, shunned, unappreciated. Raif even seems to side with his detractors. 'At home and at the office,' Sabahattin Ali writes, 'he did more than just tolerate ridicule from people with whom he had nothing in common: he seemed actively to approve of those who looked down on him.'

In depicting the unusual relationship between Maria and Raif, these two personalities from utterly different backgrounds, Ali

Ali's possessions at the time of his death.

manages to question and transcend the main dualities of his time: manhood/womanhood; East/West; tradition/modernity; rationality/ creativity. Throughout the story there is an unshakeable sense of loneliness that I cannot help but think reflected his own loneliness as he relentlessly tried to carve out a space for himself in a country that allowed little freedom of speech.

Ali was an outspoken critic, a left-leaning intellectual. Twice im-prisoned, he was always under scrutiny for his views. When, in 1948, at the age of forty-one, it became clear that he would probably be arrested again soon, he decided to leave Turkey and go to Europe. As he was crossing the border into Bulgaria he was beaten to death by the truck driver who was accompanying him — a man who, unbeknown to Ali, worked in cahoots with the Turkish secret police. The writer's body was never found.

His daughter, Filiz Ali, once said, 'My father understood love and the depth of real feelings people experience. He looked to the heart, real emotion.' This, I believe, is the main reason behind the growing popularity and allure of this book across the world. For the writer nei-ther judged nor condemned the longings of the human heart, he only wanted to understand, and in so doing, invited us, his readers, to do the same.

Ali was one of our last truly cosmopolitan intellectuals, not only a great writer but also a bridge-builder between cultures. On the last journey he took, he had very few possessions with him: a wristwatch, a notebook, a pair of glasses, a bottle of cologne, photographs of his loved ones, a copy of Balzac's *Modeste Mignon* and one of Pushkin's

Sabahattin Ali (1907–1948), here portrayed by CLYM EVERNDEN, began his career as a school teacher. He served in the military during the Second World War, was imprisoned twice for his views, and owned and edited the *Marko Paşa* newspaper. *Madonna in a Fur Coat* is his third and final novel.

Eugene Onegin. His murderer said that when he attacked him from behind, the writer was reading a book, his head buried in the pages.

I have always believed that the book Ali was reading in his last moments must have been *Eugene Onegin* — written by a man who himself was no stranger to exile and oppression, and who once notoriously said that he was 'not born to amuse the Tsars'. It is a comforting thought that perhaps somewhere, somehow, they might have found each other, our Sabahattin Ali and Russia's Alexander Pushkin, neither of them born to amuse the Tsars.

INTERVIEW

Filiz Ali, interviewed here by AYŞEGÜL SERT, is a star pianist, respected critic and all-round force for good in Turkish culture. Plus, she's the daughter of *Madonna in a Fur Coat*'s author Sabahattin Ali. After championing his work through years of censorship how must it feel to see it become so popular?

MY FATHER WROTE IT

'My father was a gentle man with endless energy who talked, walked and wrote faster than anybody I know,' Filiz Ali once wrote. Her father was Sabahattin Ali; he was killed when she was just eleven years old.

Filiz has traced a brilliant artistic path in her own right, training as a pianist and a musicologist, and making a name as an educator and critic. Her career, too vast to recount here, encompasses appearances at Istanbul State Opera, a time spent serving as artistic director of one of Istanbul's most important concert halls, Cemal Reşit Rey, and the writing of nine books, including memoirs, collections of press articles, and biographies. It is hard to keep up with Filiz Ali!

Below is our conversation from Covid-lockdown Turkey, where she continues, at the age of eighty-four, to guard her father's legacy. Filiz first read *Madonna in a Fur Coat* in her early teens. 'I especially liked it because it inspired my imagination about love,' she says. 'However, the book is more about life!'

AYŞEGÜL: Why did it take so long for your father's work to find an audience in Turkey?

FILIZ: His death and its circumstances were clouded by secret-service oppression against our family and friends. Nobody dared talk about Sabahattin Ali and his death. No publisher dared issue his books. He was doomed to be forgotten. This censorship was only eased after 1960. Thanks to my mother's commitment, his books were reissued by the publisher Varlık Yayınevi in 1965, and with our perseverance, we kept his name and his work alive throughout these years until a Sabahattin Ali renaissance emerged, thanks to the public. He became a bestseller at the age of a hundred.

A: How do you explain the younger generation's desire to read *Madonna in a Fur Coat*?

F: First, it is a good book. Its story and style are still quite fresh and real, so it moves young people's sensibilities. I do not consider it simply a love story. It is about the growing pains of a new republic being built in Turkey while also dealing with the emerging fascism during the Weimar Republic in Germany, and an unusual love story grows over this background.

A: There are uncanny parallels between what your father endured and the ordeals faced by Turkish intellectuals today.

F: I am sad to say that nothing much has changed in terms of the oppression of the state dictatorship in Turkey throughout my lifetime. Whoever dares voice opinions freely will be silenced in different ways. Freedom of expression is considered dangerous, for the good of society.

A: What made you want to become a pianist?

F: I started taking piano lessons when I was about seven years old from a Hungarian pianist who was Béla Bartók's pupil. Her name was Rozsi Szabo and she was teaching piano at the State Conservatory of Ankara, where my father was a professor. My father was killed in 1948, and I entered Ankara State Conservatory as a piano student in 1949. It was for me the most natural thing to do. The rest is a long story. I never thought of becoming a writer. However, as a musicologist, critic and musician, I wrote and still write a lot about music.

A: In *Madonna in a Fur Coat*, Raif Efendi is sent by his father from Ankara to Berlin. Sabahattin Ali also went to Berlin as a young man and those eighteen months greatly shaped his critical thinking. Can we read this novel as a mirror of its author?

F: One can easily predict that an author would use himself as the main topical material for his stories. When you read Sabahattin Ali's letters written to his friends during the 1920s and 1930s, you will find clues and similarities between his actual life and his fictional life.

A: This book was not his favourite. If Sabahattin Ali were to see its late success, what do you think would be his reaction?

F: He'd find all this attention very amusing. He would be quite happy to see that his 'novelette' has at long last found the understanding that it deserves by contemporary readers, after being neglected for so many years.

A: You've talked in the past about your belief that your father was killed by the Turkish secret police. How did you cope with that? It must have demanded a tremendous amount of courage.

F: It is not possible to describe how one is able to live and go on living after such a tragedy. Rather late in my life, I made peace with the idea of my father's death. One never forgets or forgives. I know that there is no justice in this world. However, my father lives on with his words, and his words are repeated by people speaking many different languages. Justice to his artistic legacy is done by these readers.

A: It is a heavy responsibility to carry forward a parent's legacy.

F: My mother died in 1999. I think she was very confused about my father's disappearance and possible defection to a foreign country and was devastated by his assassination. I am lucky to have a son and a daughter and two grandsons, and I hope they will carry the flag after I am gone. I never seriously thought about leaving Turkey and settling abroad. I always thought that I needed to stay and be a useful human being by transmitting what I know and what I have experienced in this life to young people. However, if I were young today, I think I'd be searching for a new life somewhere else.

EPOCH

A tragic cynicism; a sense, even in happiness, of loss. From suburban Ankara to downtown Berlin, Ali's novel offers a powerful evocation, argues DAVID SELIM SAYERS, of an atmosphere brought about by the ennui of the Lost Generation. But is its recent success linked to some equivalent shadow looming over the 2020s?

BIG CITIES CALLING

We may be witnessing the birth of a new Lost Generation. The label, famously coined by Gertrude Stein for the postwar cohort of Ernest Hemingway, has come back in fashion. Just shy of a century after its coinage, we now find it attached to a new generation, coming of age not in the shadow of a war, but of a virus. And now, just as then, the term captures more than the dwindling of economic prospects: it evokes the cultural trauma following the shutdown of an entire way of life, from politics to art, and the disorientation and disillusionment resulting from this trauma.

Enter *Madonna in a Fur Coat* by Sabahattin Ali, a Turkish interwar novel that appeared in the early 1940s, blossomed from cult classic to bestselling hit in 2010s Turkey, was greeted with rave reviews upon its 2016 English release, and has enjoyed an astonishing level of global popularity ever since. Now, in our pandemic days, the novel is more relevant than it has been at any time since its initial publication; for it offers not only an object lesson in the effects of generational trauma, but also a bold assertion of cultural creativity as the only way out and through.

When Ali wrote *Madonna in a Fur Coat*, serialised in a Turkish newspaper from 1940 to 1941, he was a soldier — one of countless men called to arms as the Second World War drew ever nearer to Turkey's borders and the country nervously braced for the worst. As history would have it, the worst was avoided, Turkey managed to protect its official neutrality, and Ali himself was discharged after four months. Still, the looming presence of the war cannot but have helped nudge him towards this remarkable Lost Generation narrative.

The story takes us back to Berlin in the Weimar Republic. Exact dates are somewhat blurry, but it seems that Raif, our protagonist, visits the German capital in the early 1920s, possibly from 1921 to 1923. The setting is anything but random: Sabahattin Ali himself had lived in Berlin, on a state scholarship to study the German language, towards the same decade's end — from 1928 to 1930, the exact period that saw the city welcome Christopher Isherwood, Stephen Spender and W. H. Auden.

Just like these three young Britons — and so many other expatriates alighting on Europe's archipelago of cultural oases in the twenties — Ali lived and wrote in the shadow of the First World War. Unlike Hemingway, eight years his senior, he'd been too young to serve in it. But unlike Auden, born in the same year as Ali, he'd grown up in the thick of it, repeatedly displaced with his family as cities fell around him and the Ottoman Empire, his proud and ancient homeland of 600 years, crumbled to dust.

CLUBBING, THEN AND NOW
Dancers at a New Year's party in a nightclub in the 1920s, and dancers at a techno party in a fetish club in the 2010s, both in Berlin.

In Turkey, the First World War, with its disgraceful undertones of genocide and defeat, is rarely remembered in its own right. Instead, it serves as mere prelude to the War of Independence (1919–1923), in which mutinous remnants of the vanquished Ottoman army rallied together, drove out Allied (mostly Greek) occupation forces from the Anatolian heartland, and founded the Republic of Turkey — a bold alchemical gesture that took the chagrin of imperial dismemberment and the shame of ethnic cleansing and transformed them into the amnesiac pride and martial glory of a modern nation-state.

In what can only be described as a stroke of literary genius, Ali sends his protagonist off to Berlin at this precise moment of alchemical transformation. Raif is out of earshot as the new nation and its heroic narrative are proclaimed. Almost uniquely among his contemporaries in Turkish fiction, he misses the siren's call. An expatriate in twenties Berlin, he remains as ideologically disillusioned—and politically apathetic—as only a true member of the Lost Generation could be. And when he finally returns home, he finds that the waste land of destruction and despair he had left behind has changed in nothing but name.

Hemingway opens *The Sun Also Rises* with the iconic Gertrude Stein quote: 'You are all a lost generation.' But he immediately parries with Ecclesiastes, 'One generation passeth away, and another generation cometh ... The sun also ariseth, and the sun goeth down, and hasteth to the place where he arose,' goading us to pick the Old Testament's fatalistic blend of resignation and hope over Stein's modernist verdict of catastrophic rupture. Yet the air of thwarted destiny and aborted life suffusing *Madonna in a Fur Coat* leaves little doubt as to which side Ali comes down on.

The loss of meaning and hope, however, are not the only attributes binding Raif to the Lost Generation. As much as the 1920s were marked by the shadow of the war, they were also lit up by a superhuman effort to leap out of this shadow through a burst of exploration and transgression in the sciences, arts, philosophy and, last but not least, lifestyle. In Berlin, it was the time of Einstein and Brecht, of Walter Benjamin and Fritz Lang, of Magnus Hirschfeld and his groundbreaking Institute of Sex Research.

Painting proved one of the most daring outlets for the transgressive spirit of the age. Fittingly, Raif first encounters his love interest Maria at an art gallery, where he dismisses the creations of avant-garde painters — with a naïve gaze worthy of Stein's Alice B. Toklas — as 'people with cubic shoulders and knees and heads and breasts of disproportionate sizes' before he breathes a sigh of relief in front of Maria's own self-portrait, reassuringly fashioned in 'the footsteps of the great masters'.

As lost a soul as any, Maria is the daughter of a Jewish man from Prague who converted to Catholicism and moved to Berlin before dying while she was still a child. She supports her painterly ambitions and ailing mother by singing and playing violin at a cabaret. It is Maria who initiates Raif into Berlin's artistic milieu. At a café they visit together, he frowns upon the clientele of 'young painters imitating the French with their long hair and pipes and their broad-rimmed black hats, and long-nailed writers leafing through their pages', a crowd straight out of Toulouse-Lautrec.

But Raif's dour rejection of the contemporary art scene makes him appear more reactionary than he truly is. For one, his stay in Berlin helps him achieve an artistic leap of his own: he abandons the romantic novels of his youth, by authors such as Alexandre Dumas and Ahmed Mithat, and turns instead to German and Russian literature, particularly the introspective, psychological work of Ivan Turgenev — a leap that pays off in the style of Raif's own memoirs, which form the bulk of *Madonna in a Fur Coat*.

More significant, though, is a cultural gift, unique to his Ottoman background, that Raif offers the Lost Generation — that of the 2020s as much as the 1920s. As opposed to fellow fictional expatriates such as *The Sun Also Rises*' Jake Barnes, Raif embodies a non-Western, non-binary take on gender. This enables him to woo Maria without any of the 'awful male pride' she so detests. But it also provides a creative response to the modern 'crisis of masculinity' that haunts Western culture from Hemingway to our day. As much as anything, it is this contribution that makes *Madonna in a Fur Coat* such a vital addition to the library of the, and any, Lost Generation.

2.2
FOUR ARTWORKS

The following series has been created by four artists responding to what is arguably the novel's most important passage, in which protagonist Raif Efendi experiences a sort of breakdown upon encountering a painting of a 'Madonna in a fur coat'. Obsessed, he'll spend days doing nothing except sitting in the gallery looking at the picture, which is a self portrait by an artist named Maria Puder. Eventually they will meet. Four artists produce their own take, their own spin, on this key encounter with a work of art. The female gaze is duly returned.

CREEPING LIKE A NUN
Julie Verhoeven

The first piece is by British artist, illustrator and designer Julie Verhoeven. Of the key passage (see below and throughout) she says: 'it's the kind of text you can wallow in like mud.' Verhoeven is known for her work with fashion brands such as Marc Jacobs and Louis Vuitton. 'The fur coat registered as down hair to me, engulfing and alluring,' she says. 'The macabre lock of hair bursting through the Fontana-esque lady slit in the canvas, was a savage untamed impression of the emotions she stirred.'

'What was it about that portrait? I know that words alone will not suffice. All I can say is that she wore a strange, formidable, haughty and almost wild expression, one that I had never seen before on a woman. But while that face was utterly new to me, I couldn't help but feel that I had seen her many times before. Surely I knew this pale face, this dark brown...

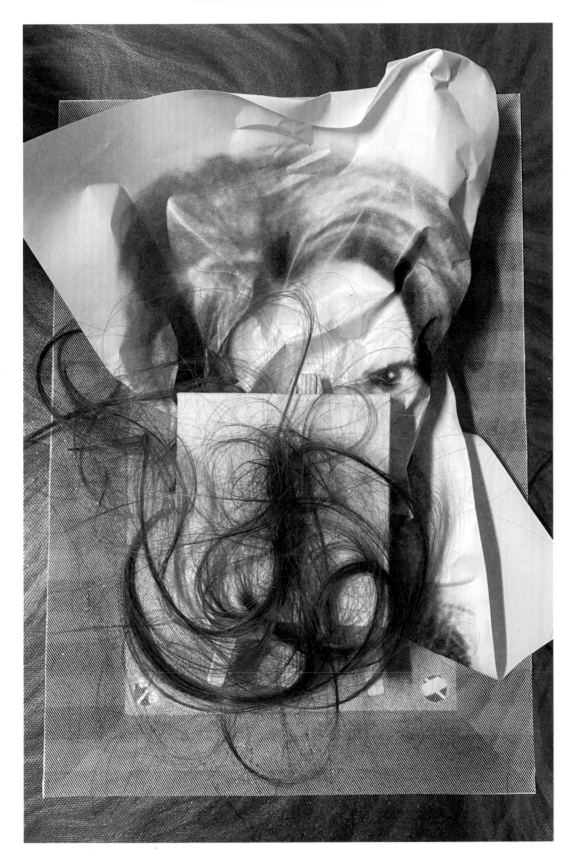

MOWA & MAXINE
Liz Johnson Artur

London-based artist Liz Johnson Artur is inspired by the way in which Raif's relationship with Maria, augured as a kind of intense premonition in the Berlin gallery, explores the meaning of both platonic and romantic love and all grey shades in between. She presents *Mowa & Maxine*, its central figures being two friends at London club night PDA. 'It reflects for me a conversation in the book about love,' says Johnson Artur. 'If a person truly has the ability to love, then he can never monopolise his beloved. When love spreads, it does not diminish. PDA was a place where love was spread like this.'

...hair, this dark brow, these dark eyes that spoke of eternal anguish and resolve. I had known that woman since I'd opened my first book at the age of seven – since I'd started, at the age of five, to dream. I saw in her echoes of Halit Ziya Uşaklıgil's Nihal, Vecihi Bey's Mehcure, and Cavalier Buridan's beloved. I saw the Cleopatra I had come to know in history books, and Muhammad's mother, Amine Hatun, of whom I had dreamed while listening to the Mevlit prayers. She was a swirling blend of all the women I had ever imagined. Dressed in...

JÎN ELMAS BERGEN
Banu Cennetoğlu

Banu Cennetoğlu first read *Madonna in a Fur Coat* thirty years ago. Even before revisiting the book she could recall the energy of Raif's encounter with the painting, the sense of being transported through the subject's eyes. 'I like Ali's work, particularly his poems,' says the Istanbul-based artist. 'A large part of it is about an eternal grief, an almost permanent state of sorrow and melancholy.'

... the pelt of a wildcat, she was mostly in shadow, but for a sliver of a pale white neck, and an oval face was turned slightly to the left. Her dark eyes were lost in thought, absently staring into the distance, drawing on a last wisp of hope as she searched for something that she was almost certain she would never find. Yet mixed in with the sadness was a sort of challenge. It was as if she were saying, "Yes, I know. I won't find what I'm looking for ... and what of it?" The same challenge was playing ...

ROXANE II
Viviane Sassen

The hidden figure is the artist's collaborator and muse, Roxane Danset. 'The image is of course in reference to the fur coat, but it goes further than that,' says Sassen. 'The woman described in the text strongly reminded me of Roxane; with her pale face, the dark brown hair and dark eyes... But especially this sentence spoke to me as it is exactly how I described Roxane in the past: "She was a swirling blend of all women I had ever imagined". Roxane truly is such a woman; a rare, classic beauty who inhabits many different women in herself; the Mother, the Child, the Madonna, the Mistress... the innocent playful, the dark, the wicked, secretive, erotic, and also the pragmatic strong motherly woman. I adore her as she keeps on inspiring me.'

...on her plump lips. The lower lip was slightly fuller. Her eyelids were somewhat swollen. Her eyebrows were neither thick nor thin but short. The dark-brown hair that framed her broad forehead fell down over her cheeks, and her fur coat. Her pointed chin was slightly upturned. Her nose was long, her nostrils flared. My hands were almost trembling as I flipped through the exhibition catalogue. I was hoping I might find out more about the painting. At the bottom of a page at the very end, I found just three words beside the number of the painting: Maria Puder, *Selbstporträt*. Nothing else.'

2.3
APPENDIX

Footnotes on phenomena relating to Raif and Maria. To summarise: In Ankara in the 1930s an unnamed narrator becomes fascinated by a colleague. This is Raif. He wears knit vests and lives in an unremarkable suburban house but is secretly an artist of quite some skill. They become friends, and when Raif falls ill he says: please can you destroy the black notebook I keep in my desk in the office? Of course, the narrator reads it instead. It contains a beautifully-written memoir recalling an episode which occurred in the early 1920s. Raif is sent to Berlin by his stern father after dropping out of art school, and lives for a while in a cabbagey-smelling hotel on Lützowstraße. He is meant to learn about soap manufacturing. Instead he spends his time going to galleries, reading books, and drinking in beer halls, at least until he befriends the woman he believes is the love of his life. That's Maria. To begin they simply wander around Berlin together, such as to the botanical gardens in the south west of the city...

ON THE LAST SENTENCE
by Tim Blanks

'Placing his black notebook before me, I turned back to the first page.'

I read the end of a book first. It started as an effort to save myself from something I wasn't enjoying. If I was intrigued by the last chapter, maybe I would have an incentive to persevere. But then I found that, once I knew where I was going, I enjoyed getting there a lot more. The upside: I don't waste time investing in things I can tell won't be rewarding. The caveat: I'm a deeply flawed individual, lazy with terrible time management skills.

ON BERLIN BOTANICAL GARDENS
by Jan Kedves

'We returned to the botanical gardens several times and twice we went to the opera in the evening.'

Longing to reconnect with nature, the contemporary traveller hops on a plane and flies to distant, less populated lands (at least before the pandemic). In Berlin, a drive out southwest to Botanischer Garten is enough. Wedged in between the boroughs of Dahlem, Steglitz and Lichterfelde, this 430,000-square-metre triangle showcases the entire globe's natural plant diversity in imposing greenhouses and in an arboretum (i.e. outdoor tree collection), traversed by smoothly curving pathways. The rich display of flora here even features some fauna in the form of foxes that, in true fashion of half-domesticated city foxes, are quite tame, almost bowing and scraping around visitors' ankles.

Before Botanischer Garten first opened to the public in 1903, this patch of land was used as potato fields. Berliners have since enjoyed the place for a welcome escape, come sunshine, rain or snow. Over 20,000 species from all over the world are on display, and linguistically versed plant-lovers have a field day perusing all sorts of cheeky names on the identification signs: there's *Sarcococca hookeriana*, a low-growing evergreen shrub also known as Himalayan sweet box; there's *Adonis*

amurensis, also known as pheasant's eye, a perennial plant with a golden yellow flower that in Japan is known as *Fukujusō*, which translates as 'fortune longevity plant'. Lovers of the clematis might, within just a few steps under a large pergola for woody climbers, be pleased to find the *tubulosa*, *integrifolia*, *hexapetala* and *recta* variants. It's all a real parade-slash-paradise of photosynthesis.

Yet, when Sabahattin Ali processed his own experience of the city in *Madonna in a Fur Coat*, he added a grain of sadness to his description. Maria tells Raif that Botanischer Garten is 'the most beautiful place in Berlin', while, on one of their joint walks through the garden, adding: 'these strange trees always remind me of all the faraway lands I long to see... I pity them, you know — for having been uprooted from their natural soil and brought here to be grown under artificial conditions.'

Can plants become homesick? Is Berlin really 'a kind of torture' for them, as Maria claims? To be honest, walking through Botanischer Garten in 2021 leaves no doubt that even the most exotic plants have adapted well to their German surroundings. Even the lanky *Metasequoia glyptostroboides*, a fast-growing,

endangered conifer from the remote Chinese provinces of Sichuan and Hubei, thrives here as those potatoes once did. In fact, the potato was uprooted, too, from the Andean heights of Peru, Chile and Bolivia, but it has become so indigenous to German soil and German cuisine that the very natives of this land are now, lovingly and sardonically, referred to as *Kartoffeln*, potatoes. All to say that, rather than getting too gloomy and philosophical about roots, one could just revel in the abundant display of biodiversity or in the thought that nature is at home wherever it is.

ON THE KNIT VEST
by Hilal Isler

'Here was a man who guarded his health most jealously, who wrapped himself up in layer after layer of woollen vests and pullovers'

The knit vest — or *yelek* — has dominated the fashion landscape of Turkish men since antiquity, flattering those with a *rakı* [Turkish liquor] gut or *börek* [filled pastry] belly with a neutral, visually slimming effect, and offering, I would argue, the purest distillation of Turkish masculine energy in existence.

Usually v-neck, cable knit, and worn over a long, collared shirt, Turkish *yelek*s

are pulled out of the dresser at the very first sign of autumn, and worn straight through to the end of March. In the event that the *yelek* has been preserved with naphthalene mothballs, the garment is aired out on the balcony for at least 24 hours before use. It is a Turkish childhood rite of passage to mistake a mothball for a stray Mentos candy and, upon swallowing, to be rushed to the nearest emergency medical facility.

The Turkish sweater vest can be paired with thick corduroy pants to complete the look of off-duty lumberjack, or a man fully prepared to embark on a fishing expedition with no notice. Houndstooth, v-neck, cable knit, the *yelek* has been mass-produced by Turkish textile manufacturers — such as Vakko and Beymen — for generations. But more valuable are the ones lovingly knit by grandmothers across the nation or, more recently, by non-binary craft enthusiasts on Etsy.

ON LÜTZOWSTRAßE
by Rob Doyle

'"Where do you live?" "On Lützow Street."'

I'm about to walk the length of Lützowstraße for what I imagine will be the first and last time — not just because I'm leaving Berlin in a couple of days, but because there usually isn't much to bring me out to this part of the city: the area of Mitte south of Tiergarten.

Earlier today I tested negatively for Covid-19 at a former fetish club on the other side of town; when I land at Dublin airport I can present the certificate and avoid being directed to a hotel to quarantine for two weeks. I've been counting the days till I get out of Berlin — not a sentence I ever imagined I'd write. For weeks there's been no sunlight, though today the sky is cold blue above the lines of balconies and under-construction blocks as I turn onto the quiet street. I'm known to bang on about how much I love grey skies and the sombre side of the year, yet two out of the four winters I've spent in Berlin I've fallen into a more or less deep depression. This plague-winter, *everyone* is depressed, looking for someone to blame. Last weekend the Dutch rioted in the streets, torching cars and fighting cops. The

uprising seemed under-reported on the news sites, as if the press didn't want to give the rest of us any ideas.

Not having eaten since breakfast, I cast a hunter's eye on both sides of Lützowstraße for promising take-outs, something I can eat with cold hands and no fuss. I pass a couple of shabby hotels, their facades warmed by shafts of sunlight that lance between the rooftops. The worst hotels are always the ones that seem to me the most romantic, pregnant with mystery. These aren't hotels for tourists: they're the kind where men in cheap suits check in and are found the next morning, hanging from the shower fixtures; where women from countries no one cares about come to bad ends. Indeed, they're not far off the kind of establishment that in old novels are called 'pensions' — like the one on this street where the young Raif Efendi lived, batting off the drunken advances of a thirty-something widow renting an adjacent room.

Passing the hotels, I'm surprised to spot Kumpelnest 3000 — so I *have* been on this street before — a queer bar of long-standing repute where my friend Alex-Alvina took me one raucous night a year ago. Even by Berlin standards it was packed, smoky, glittering, wild. By the end of the night Alex-Alvina was dancing on the tables, and I was sharing lines with a stranger in a cubicle, later to realise he was bar staff. Now Kumpelnest has the forlorn look of every bar and club in Berlin, haunted by the ghost of all the fun that's been had here, the music and the sweat. A 'Bars of Berlin' poster in the window reads *OHNE UNS IST BERLIN NUR NOCH ARM*. 'Without us, Berlin is only poor' — a faintly passive-aggressive allusion to the city's louche motto.

At the corner of Potsdamer Straße I buy a coffee and a burger. I eat while standing on the street, across from a strip club and yet more sleazy hotels. The declining afternoon sun shines directly down Potsdamer Straße and I let it flood into me, fancying I can discern the pulse of serotonin, or Vitamin D, or whatever it is we need in winter when our thoughts turn to suicide hotels, to burning it all down, to going to seed. Meanwhile, a man approaches, improbably dressed in the same precise and bygone get-up — black fedora, long coat, suit — as the sadistic Gestapo villain in *Raiders of the Lost Ark*: a film, I hereby confess, that I lately rewatched in the suspicion that it contained hidden-in-plain-sight truths about the nature of the Nazis' occult fixation. He is pulling a black wheeled suitcase (carrying the Staff of Ra? the Spear of Destiny?). I finish my burger and cross Potsdamer Straße.

On I walk, past a closed traditional restaurant called Joseph-Roth-Diele (which looks like it's been here since Roth's journalistic Berlin heyday in the 1920s) till I reach the green and sculpture-specked Lützow Platz, the terminus of the street. I sit for a while on a bench, in the low hum of traffic that flows around the hotel-lined square. Later this evening, when I'm back home and my fingers are warm enough to google, I'll learn that in one of these buildings, on 25 February 1932, Adolf Hitler was granted German citizenship. With that bureaucratic chore out of the way, Hitler would go on — famously — to overturn German democracy, spread chaos across Europe and wage total war. The rest is history, and me sitting on Lützow Platz in the slant winter light, wondering if I'll ever be here again.

ON BACKGAMMON
by Sevil Delin

'By now I'd come to know some of the clerks from other departments well enough to go out with them to a coffee house in the evenings to play backgammon.'

Although both coffee and backgammon are imports to Turkey (coffee from Yemen, backgammon from Persia), they have become intrinsic parts of its culture and definitions of

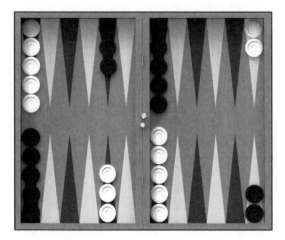

masculinity. Backgammon is known as *tavla* in Turkish, derived from the Latin *tabula*, also the root of the word 'table' (similar to the term 'board game'). The Turkish word for coffee, *kahve*, refers to both the drink itself and to where it is drunk: the coffeehouse, an Ottoman conception. Across Turkey, from villages to metropolises, coffeehouses are solely the realm of men, places between the stultifying worlds of work and home where they can unwind and reveal their true nature. Backgammon is often the arena for this bombastic posturing, accompanied by much theatrics, joviality — and profanity. The board, like chess, is a virtual battlefield where men play at war. When an experienced, older player defeats a more junior opponent, it is traditional for him to slam the board shut, tuck it under the arm of the loser, and humiliate him by adding, '*Öğren de gel*': 'Learn how to play, and only then come back.' Persian numbers are still used, and have crossed over into the lexicon: *duşeş* means 'double sixes' in Persian (the best possible combination you can roll) and has come to mean 'a serendipitous windfall'. Conversely, *hep yek* means 'always one' — the worst roll of the dice — and implies a series of misfortunes.

Women have historically been excluded from both the coffeehouse and from playing backgammon, unless it's at home and the version condescendingly known as *kız tavlası* ('girls' backgammon'), a simplified form that removes any elements of strategy, reducing it to a game of chance. Since the 1990s, however, as a greater number of young Turkish women have entered university and, subsequently, the workforce, one symbolic field they have conquered is the backgammon board, joining their male counterparts in student coffeehouses and taking up the dice.

ON SOAP MANUFACTURING
by Richard Godwin

'So as not to tell my father an outright lie, I managed, with the help of several Turkish friends, to present myself to a manufacturer of luxury soap.'

In Babylon one evening, a certain person noticed something bubbling in the embers of their fire. Or it might have happened in Nineveh. It's impossible to know. But somewhere in ancient Mesopotamia, it was observed that when animal fat is mixed with ash from a fire it creates a lather — and when this lather is mixed with water, it has remarkable cleaning properties.

This was the first soap: oil + alkali + water. The first recorded mention comes from 2800BC. Soap was widely used in antiquity. In ancient Egypt, it was made from cypress oil and ash; Phoenician soaps were made of tallow and beech ash; and Aleppo soap is made to this day by boiling olive oil, lye (sodium hydroxide) and water for three days, adding some laurel oil, pouring the liquid into a mould, leaving it to harden, cutting it into cubes and leaving these to breathe for seven months. It comes out a lovely waxy green. It's apparently more effective at destroying coronavirus than hand sanitiser.

The Romans used soap for washing clothes but considered washing themselves with it barbaric, preferring the oil-and-scrape method. But it was the Romans who gave us the word,

sapo, a borrowing from the Celtic *saipo*, tallow, i.e. animal fat.

The modern Turkish word is *sabun*. In the fourteenth century, Arab and Persian chemists honed production methods and newer, less abrasive soaps became an Ottoman speciality. There are excellent, cheap handmade olive-oil soaps available all over Turkey, stamped by the manufacturer and perfumed with rose, chamomile and thyme. The city of Edirne was once famous for its fruit-scented soaps, which were shaped to look like cherries, apples, peaches and lemons and sent to the palace of the Sultan.

For the most part, Westerners held on to quasi-Roman attitudes to soap until surprisingly recently; Muslim travellers to Europe often marvelled at the filthiness of the natives. However, once it had been established that soap was a good way to use up surplus animal fat from meat-packing, and that soap killed germs, a market was created. William Procter and James Gamble founded their soap-and-candle company in Cincinnati in 1837 and supplied the North with soap during the American Civil War. In Britain, the Lever Brothers were the first to exploit new industrial methods of making soap by combining palm oil and glycerine. By 1888, they were selling 450 tons a week.

To sell this amount of soap, the soap companies needed to convince people that they were dirty in ways that hadn't worried them before, and so soap and advertising co-evolved. Soap operas are called soap operas because they were first funded by soap companies to create opportunities to advertise soap. And it turned out that the war on dirt could never be won. Once white, clothes had to be whiter than white. P&G and Unilever are now among the world's largest corporations.

ON A FUR COAT
by Gert Jonkers

'I dashed off after the Madonna in a Fur Coat, hoping I might catch her.'

One Saturday night in New York City, 22 October 2005, we were out to party. One of us knew we had to be at Misshapes, a night at West Village disco Luke & Leroy's. Some superstar was possibly going to preview her upcoming album. Half of New York had picked up on the rumour, but some of us must have had friends at the door. Our little party pack included Mel, a stylist who went on to head *Interview* magazine; Jeppe, who would write gay-pride anthem 'Born This Way' for Lady Gaga; James, who now runs a fancy B&B in Orbetello, Tuscany; Felix, founder of *Pin-Up*, a magazine for architectural entertainment; Jason, who used to lavish us with pairs of Converse shoes; and my colleague Jop — we had just launched the second issue of *Fantastic Man* earlier that week. The venue was tiny and packed. The music was super pumpy. We recognised the nerdy-looking young man behind the turntables as Stuart Price. That was a sign. Security paced around nervously. Lights flashing, the air went electric; Apple hadn't launched its iPhone yet so I stuck out my little digital camera. And in walked Madonna in a fur coat.

ON CABBAGEY WHIFF
by Rosa Rankin-Gee

'Returning to the pension in the evening, I'd catch my first whiff of cabbage from a distance of a hundred paces.'

Cabbage that the human nostril can discern at 100 paces, that is to say approximately 250 ft or 76.2 meters, will certainly have been the recipient of a good long boil. On heating, and particularly on heating at length, sulphur compounds in cabbage become volatile and convert into molecules including dimethyl disulphide and hydrogen sulphide — the artist also known as 'rotten-eggs smell'.

Heavier than air, hydrogen sulphide tends to spread its whiffs and wafts along the ground, thus the intrepidness of its travel. It is rarely discussed — including in scientific papers — without the qualifier 'extremely pungent'.

Bulky and iron-rich, cabbages took a starring role across both world wars and the interwar years. To the Allies, before they became 'Jerries' or 'Fritzes', the Germans were 'Krauts', and upon America's entry into the conflict, sauerkraut got the treatment that would later befall the French fry: it was renamed 'liberty cabbage'. Cabbage also found its way into role-playing: in Weimar Republic Berlin, at roughly the period in time when the novel's principal action takes place, it seems that ersatz black-market 'cigars' were made from cabbage leaves marinated in nicotine.

At night in the brassica-infused pension, Raif recounts reading incessantly. If, as he mentions, he read all Turgenev's stories in a single sitting, we might imagine him also coming across the Russian author's short prose poem 'Shchi', or 'Cabbage Soup'. In it, a widowed peasant woman whose son has died is watched with horror by the rich landlady of the village, as she ladles spoonful after spoonful of cabbage soup into her mouth. 'My God, Tatjana! Did you not love your son? How can you eat cabbage soup at a time like this?' the rich woman asks. The bereaved widow is in despair but nevertheless, on she eats. 'The head of my living body has been taken away from me!' she replies. '… But is that any reason for not eating the soup? It is nicely salted.'

ON INDESCRIBABLE TORRENTS OF EMOTION IN GALLERIES
by Stephen Curtis

'Even now, after all these years, I cannot describe the torrent that swept through me in that moment.'

I have been granted intimate access to the lives of strangers. I, like my fellow gallery workers the world over, have witnessed art wasting space and working magic. Art orchestrating the rhythm of crowds, whispering in the ear of the solitary viewer. Art greeted with suspicion or derision, awe and observance. I have seen visitors recoiling in protest or sitting, heads bowed in contemplation, hands clasped together or, increasingly, swiping, texting. Lovers kissing, maybe meeting for the first time. People stripped bare, claiming to be spiritually moved by overtly secular works; Arthur Jafa on race or late Rothko have opened wounds as deep as a Grünewald or Caravaggio. Is there not a quasi-religious pulse beating in all who swoon before what they perceive to be great or outstanding contributions to culture? Specifically those who return over and over in order to worship at the home of their *idée fixe*, be that chapel, gallery or gilded palace. Many modern-day pilgrims are stunned into silence before the object of their adoration, but a small number it seems are mysteriously changed, psychologically disorientated by what they have seen, what they have experienced — the principal symptoms of which appear to be consistent with the tropes of devotional iconography: fainting, inner conflict, ecstasy.

Dr Graziella Magherini, a psychiatrist at Santa Maria Nuova hospital in Florence was the first to detect and analyse the condition of tourists requiring medical attention having been exposed to the art and architecture of Florence. In 1989 she gave it a name: Stendhal Syndrome. Stendhal was the nom-de-plume of French writer Marie-Henri Beyle, who in 1817 described an almost out-of-body experience on visiting the tombs of Galileo, Michelangelo and Machiavelli at Basilica di Santa Croce, Florence. In his travel journal (Naples & Florence: A Journey from Milan to Reggio) Stendhal claimed his very soul had been in a trance and he had succumbed to what he believed to be celestial sensations. Stendhal Syndrome, also known as Florence Syndrome or dissociative transitory amnesia results in tourists losing their composure, their way or even their mind after too much of a good thing, namely the Renaissance.

On hearing of Stendhal's account, my first thought was would it be possible now in this desolate age, our precarious ecology, to give credence to such hysteria, such oxygen-deprived reactions to so-called great art, not least in an epoch relentlessly rethinking and reconfiguring the canon? Evidently so, as there have indeed been hundreds of cases of tourists passing out, giving in to varying degrees of ecstasy or apoplexy (dizziness, confusion, even heart attack) before a Botticelli or a Giotto. Is this art fugue within reach only when one is away from home, transported? Does one have to be stationed beneath the sacred and profane *in the flesh*, or would it be equally possible to attain this altered state of absorption by catching a glimpse of an exhibition poster from a passing subway train or merely handling a postcard reproduction in a museum gift store?

As the pandemic recedes tourists will once again be buzzing or bored in galleries across the globe, but in Florence they will continue to faint. In the city viewed by many as the zenith of culture, grace and geometry, even a portal to the divine, a number of tourists will inevitably struggle to keep it together and forget to breathe.

It is essential of course to question any clichéd causal link between art and madness; however, is it not also tempting in this uncanny twilight to invite the possibility that at the right time and in the right space we may also be suffocated by beauty and seduced against our will. With good reason love has been described as a sickness. Submission to this maelstrom can lead to obsession and all too often tragedy. Perhaps love takes its purest form in the moments *before* the revelation. In the case of unrequited love for an object or image fixed forever in time, are we not bound to return over and over to this moment? That first sighting, the birth of love. Which if nothing else saves us from disappointment.

ON AHMET MITHAT EFENDI
by *Hilal Isler*

'It was the authors I read — Michel Zevaco, Jules Verne, Alexandre Dumas, Ahmet Mithat Efendi and Vecihi Bey — who painted my imagination.'

The Ottoman novelist, editor and publisher Ahmet Mithat Efendi started his professional life as an apprentice at an herbalist stall inside the Grand Bazaar, where he was beaten regularly. Having escaped that situation, with the help of a prominent statesman, he went on to launch what would be one of the most important newspapers in Istanbul, the *Tercüman-i Hakîkat*, chronicling life during the final four decades of the Ottoman Empire.

Today, Ahmet Mithat is perhaps most remembered for his iconic novel *Felâtun Bey and Râkim Efendi*, which was translated into English for the first time in 2016. The story follows Felâtun, an Ottoman dandy or "züppe", a superficially modernised male bimbo who frequents casinos and likes to sleep around, and Râkim, who lives a middle-class life defined by earnest hard work, thrift, and intellectual engagement, embodying the ideal of what Mithat Efendi believed the Ottoman Empire should strive for: a society where modernisation hasn't stopped at the surface, and hasn't just been reduced to mindless consumerism and sex. In this way, Felâtun and Râkim serve as a metaphor for what the Empire was going through at the time; the Turkish people — then as now — forever calibrating, balancing their lives between pressures European, Western, and those more rooted in tradition and faith.

ON DELICIOUSLY DRY RHEIN WINE
by Aaron Ayscough

'I was astonished to see how quickly she knocked back the glasses of the deliciously dry Rhein wine that they kept bringing to our table.'

Readers with an interest in German wine might note that the 'deliciously dry Rhein wine' would have born little resemblance to the Rheinhessen's most famous export, the evocatively-named Liebfrauenmilche ('Beloved Lady's Milk'), a sweet wine from the Muller-Thurgau grape that saw huge international success from the 1950s to the 1980s in the form of the Blue Nun wine brand.

Was Rhein wine simply drier back then?

Sort of. Sugar addition was already common in this northerly region. But contemporary sweet winemaking, as a technological phenomenon, had yet to occur. Wine wasn't sold in a sterile state, so residual yeasts and bacteria would continue to consume sugars even in the bottle. Sterile membrane filtration technology would arrive in 1926, becoming common in German winemaking by the 1940s, thus permitting the miraculous biological stabilisation — and mass export — of sweet wines like Blue Nun.

'After the war the Rheinhessen totally lost the plot,' observes winemaker Andi Mann, part of a new generation of natural winemakers working to restore quality winemaking

in the Rheinhessen. 'Chaptalisation [adding sugar to increase alcohol content] was a big thing. And most vineyards here can be mechanised. So winegrowers really tried to make high yields with machines.'

The dynamic wasn't limited to the Rheinhessen. After the Second World War, membrane filtration undergirded a late-twentieth-century global fad for overcropped, chaptalised, sterile-filtered sweet wines. Alongside Blue Nun, there was Cold Duck, White Zinfandel, Riunite Lambrusco, and more. The lingering cultural memory of such wines is why almost everyone nowadays claims to prefer dry wine.

In the Rheinhessen today, natural winemakers like Mann are forswearing chemical fertilisers, chaptalisation, and filtration, spearheading a return to the vivacious, low-alcohol, 'deliciously dry' styles of yesteryear. Climate change has obviated the rationale for chaptalisation — and for the early-ripening, low-acid Muller-Thurgau grape behind Blue Nun.

'We've always been a cool climate place, so warmer temperatures aren't bad for us,' says Mann. 'But we need acidity to have a good fermentation. So now everyone is talking about Riesling.'

ON THE SITTING ROOM
by Hilal Isler

'The girl took me into the sitting room. Here, too, the furnishings were fine, even expensive.'

The Turkish formal sitting room, in my experience, is an area none of the home's regular occupants are allowed to set foot in, let alone use, unless guests are present. Once received, such guests — the *misafir* — are invited to settle into the velvet, between numerous decorative pillows, and spend a moment admiring the doilies. They're then left to enjoy the wall clock's hypnotic ticking, as the hosts scramble in the kitchen, taking turns trying to lift the crystal decanter (each family unit must own one heavy crystal drink set, including a giant decanter nobody can actually lift).

It is a timeless Turkish tradition to ask that guests eat as much as they humanly can, repeatedly and aggressively insisting they do so, to the point that the guests feel physically threatened. Protests such as 'I am gluten intolerant' or 'I'm actually really allergic to nuts' must be either mocked or completely ignored by the hosts. It's important to note: if guests leave without a moderate case of gastritis, the whole visit will be considered a failure.

ON BODY LANGUAGE
by Seb Emina

'I was constantly being brought up short by this new habit among people my age and younger: seeing a stranger for the first time, they'd look at him with blatant curiosity as if they'd never seen anything like him.'

Expressions of body language go in and out of fashion all the time. Some become famous such as, in the 1990s, the 'Arsenio Hall fist pump', an enthusiastic rotation of the fist by the side of the head coined by the American talk show host. More recently there's scrunching up a fist, palm-side down, then abruptly opening it, the all-pervasive 'mic drop'.

Most gesture fads are harder to track, though, being subconscious imitations rather than knowing performances. A certain sassy way of smiling, a quick one-two arch of the eyebrow, a wonky configuration of mean glare: these sweep through a community for a few months then vanish too quickly for anyone to actually name them, let alone for anthropologists to write them down, and certainly not for emoji committees to put them on a custom keyboard.

The realm of the emoji is, nonetheless, a transformative force as to ways of watching body language. It makes the online equivalent of gesture trends completely visible, for example the fashion for using the 'face with monocle' graphic to create the exact equivalent of *Madonna in a Fur Coat*'s 'looking at person with blatant curiosity as if you've never seen anything like them'. Yet what started as an attempt to mimic real-world body language in the online space is now exerting an influence in the opposite direction. See for example how the shrugging of shoulders is mostly done in an exaggerated way, hands out by shoulders, eyebrows raised to a cartoonish height, a performative, if usually subconscious, imitation of the corresponding emoji.

ON BAVARIAN OUTFITS
by Jamie MacRae

'A woman dressed in a traditional Bavarian outfit and with hair like corn tassels was belting out a cheerful mountain folk song as she twirled about.'

For example the dirndl — that uniquely folky and very German assembly of bodice, skirt, blouse and apron. It is a difficult outfit to do in a 'modern' way, with attempts ending up looking either seedy and fetishy (see those made from leather or satin), or overly bright and incredibly tacky, like those cheap three-piece suits adorned with love hearts or snowmen worn by men of a certain age and paunch on stag dos. Thus, convention is best. Go for maxi rather than mini in terms of hemline, deep and rich in terms of colour, and eschew man-made fabrics for fine cottons, linens and velvet. Anything less might require a visit from *die Modepolizei*.

ON AN ACADEMY OF FINE ARTS
by Kaya Genç

'During my months at the Academy of Fine Arts in Istanbul, a few of my friends had taken dance lessons from the White Russians who were everywhere in the city at that time.'

Raif's father brands his son effeminate, dreamy, useless. He wounds Raif beyond repair, forcing him to flee for Berlin. To realise what such fathers have been doing to sensitive young Turks a century on, we should look at Istanbul's Fine Arts Academy, a sanctuary for damaged artists like Raif.

In Turkish, the Academy is called *Mekteb-i Sanayi-i Nefise-i ōahane*. At its opening in

1883 it comprised an atelier and five class-rooms. Twenty students enrolled. White Russian models, on the run from Bolshevism, were employed as nudes. Wine was served during lunchtime, *à la française*.

Raif is typically tightlipped about his time there. Fearful of his future, he drifts. But not on the canvas. 'I only ever presented my most trivial efforts,' he writes. 'If my works expressed anything personal, or exposed any personal particularity, I went to extreme lengths to hide them away, lest they ever see the light of day.'

I live near the Academy's current campus, which is located by the sea; each time I pass by the Academy buildings I ponder Raif's studentship. A tram rattles past me; young Academy students, with piercings and pastel-pink hair, roll cigarettes while passing through the metal gate.

What if he graduated, and went to Berlin not to learn soap-making but to advance his drawing skills? What if that aloof man who fantasised about becoming a famous painter touring Europe overcame his 'old silence' and learned to deal with it artistically? Had that fantasist learned to pour himself onto his canvases, and confided in them, the same way he did with Maria Puder, what would be the result? What if that terrifically unhappy youth used his colour palette, and embraced his reputation as a 'young girl' and reappropriated it as a queer artist?

A fire in 1948 destroyed the Academy's archive. Twelve-thousand books and paintings were reduced to ashes. Like its fictional lapsed student Raif, the Academy never escaped tides of ill fortune. Still I dream of finding Raif's Academy drawings one day, and of poring over the fruits of his labours. A sensitive soul, too shy for self-exposure, but too gifted for self-concealment, would then return to me in another black notebook, this one filled with Raif's art.

ON BEER HALLS
by Rob Doyle

'One day she invited me out for an afternoon stroll and on our way back she talked me into stopping at a beer hall, where we drank enough to lose track of the time.'

Beer halls weren't really a factor in my experience of life in Berlin — actually, I'm not sure such venues are even to be found in the city these days, or ever were. I suspect that the brief beer-hall scene in *Madonna in a Fur Coat* is the product of authorial licence or misre-membering. When I think of beer halls I think of Munich, and Bavaria, and of course the Beer Hall Putsch.

What *was* a factor in my time in Berlin was drinking beer (and wine and spirits and Sekt) in the countless bars and *Kneipen* whose closure this winter has made Berlin the most tantalising, melancholy of cities in which to sit out the pandemic.

There's one *Kneipe* — that is, an unpre-tentious locals' boozer, north Germany's answer to southern beer halls — that holds urban-myth status as the bar that stayed open, uninterruptedly, for some thirty years. Bei Schlawinchen, just off Kottbusser Damm in Kreuzberg, is the name of this smoked-up, rowdy *Kneipe*, where you could drink beer and inevitably chat with randomers of all stripes — vest-wearing mulleted proles, flamboyant queers, clubbers coming up or down, hen parties, svelte art-weirdos, punks — any time of day or night, all year long.

The possibly apocryphal story I heard was that even when somebody was once murdered on the premises, the owners kept it open, letting the cops cordon off the crime scene while the drinkers came and went around them.

During the first lockdown, which I spent in Ireland, a friend posted a photo of Schlawinchen with its shutters down and door locked. It felt like seeing a legendary heavyweight fighter knocked to the floor.

LETTERS

Sweet coffee clarifications, and peace to all ghosts

Hello Happy Reader,

In *THR15*, footnote (sidenote?) no. 4 in the Sarah Jessica Parker interview regarding New York City coffee vernacular is not entirely correct, or complete. The rules below generally apply to ordering a cup of coffee at a deli/corner store/bodega, not Starbucks or any kind of fancy artisanal coffee shop, and are based on my nearly thirty years of observation and NYC coffee consumption.

– A 'regular' coffee is always made with milk, never cream (unless you ask), and about one to two heaping teaspoons of sugar.
– A 'light and sweet' coffee is indeed made with 'absurd amounts' of sugar and lots of milk. In the East Village, my friends also called it 'heroin coffee' or 'crack coffee', because it was favoured by the local drug addicts.
– Other options are 'black' (no milk, no sugar), 'light' (milk, no sugar), 'extra-light' (more milk, no sugar) and 'black and sweet' (black, with one to two or more heaping teaspoons of sugar).

Anywhere else in the US you'll only be offered cream for your coffee at diners, fast food joints and most restaurants. You have to ask specifically for milk, which can mean someone running to the kitchen or stooping behind the counter to open a jug of milk and pouring some in a juice glass for your New York City ass.

Andy Reynolds
New York City, USA

Dear Happy Reader,

I was so excited when you wanted to talk about *Japanese Ghost Stories*. We tend to think that ghost stories are only for children. In reality, when we are getting older, we will find more ghosts around us: the ghosts of our past, the ghosts of our dead relatives. It makes me think that we cannot fight or deny it, but rather we should live with it and make peace out of it. I hope we all find the peace we are looking for in this world.

Best regards,
Ajrina Rarasrum
Yogyakarta, Indonesia

Dear Happy Reader,

I was a toddler when the first seasons of *Sex and the City* came out, and likely still far younger than HBO's target demographic when my sister and I would race home from school to watch sporadic, illicit reruns in the early aughts. But before I was old enough to formulate a critical opinion of the show, the women on screen were sexy, sophisticated and intriguing, and *Sex and the City* was cemented as my 'comfort' binge-watch. To witness Sarah Jessica Parker grace last issue's cover had me release an audible 'eek' of excitement. But as I read her interview, I realised the folly of my Carrie Bradshaw-based expectations. On some level I was thinking it'd be an interview in which a freelance writer funds an Upper East Side apartment and a strappy Manolo Blahnik sandal for every occasion. Instead, I was able to glimpse the flip side of the sparkling cosmopolitan we all see in Parker. My absolute favourite part was the story of her first apartment, a 'Coming to New York' narrative that is at once easier to digest than Carrie Bradshaw's dumb luck and random affluence, and a sad memorial of a friend. It was an unexpected change to separate Parker from her fame and the iconic show, if only for an interview.

All the best,
Elise Hyrak
Edmonton, Canada

Tell us what we got wrong or any interesting trajectory we've sent you off on by writing to the *Happy Reader* inbox on letters@thehappyreader.com.

Let's do this. Let's read *Middlemarch*. That sprawling English novel will be Book of the Season for the next *Happy Reader*, the globally ambient book club you are holding in your hand.

NOW IT'S MIDDLEMARCH O'CLOCK

George Eliot's 900-page novel *Middlemarch: A Study of Provincial Life* tends to be accompanied by phrases like 'but it's just so long' from those who haven't read it, and 'the best novel in the English language' from those who have.

It's a surprise page-turner, saturated with timeless wisdom that often has the reader laughing out loud. All is centred around the community of Middlemarch, a fictional English town somewhere in the Midlands (also the region in which Mary Ann Evans, the great woman behind the George Eliot pen name, was born). The true facts of history are a backdrop, but the twists and turns of human relationships are key. Virginia Woolf described it as 'one of the few English novels written for grown-up people'.

Despite being published in 1871, people are really talking about *Middlemarch* right now almost as if it were a new discovery. This is partly because, like the other weighty doorstop novels written by the likes of Tolstoy and Proust, this is a book that people have finally picked up during this past year's relentless home time. But is there more to it than that? Aren't we now at an opportune moment to think about the themes it explores, especially as rendered in this context of an Englishness that is so — how to put it — fidgety right now?

Perhaps you're personally at the vanguard of *Middlemarch* mania. Perhaps you're achingly curious so feel fine to schlep it around for a while. Either way, there will be much for you to enjoy in the seventeenth issue of the magazine, and we'd love to hear your thoughts on any aspect of the novel, no matter how small, at letters@thehappyreader.com.

SUBSCRIBE

The Happy Reader is a magazine for readers, about reading, known for its carefully chosen interviews and snazzy excavations into great works of literature. Subscribe and receive it right there on your doormat by visiting thehappyreader.com.

For something to browse in between print editions, *Happy Readings* is a free email newsletter delivered monthly and compiled by *The Happy Reader*'s editor-in-chief. To receive the bookish news, reading recommendations and very small interviews it offers, sign up directly at thehappyreader.com/newsletter.

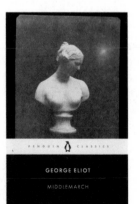

GEORGE ELIOT

MIDDLEMARCH

Jacket for *Middlemarch*, originally published in 1871.